MAD LIBS
An imprint of Penguin Random House LLC
1745 Broadway, New York, New York 10019

First published in the United States of America as *Gobble Gobble Mad Libs* by Mad Libs, an imprint of Penguin Random House LLC, 2013

This edition published by Mad Libs, an imprint of Penguin Random House LLC, 2025

Mad Libs format and text copyright © 2013, 2025 by Penguin Random House LLC

Concept created by Roger Price & Leonard Stern

Cover illustration by Skyler Kratofil

Penguin Random House values and supports copyright. Copyright fuels creativity, encourages diverse voices, promotes free speech, and creates a vibrant culture. Thank you for buying an authorized edition of this book and for complying with copyright laws by not reproducing, scanning, or distributing any part of it in any form without permission. You are supporting writers and allowing Penguin Random House to continue to publish books for every reader. Please note that no part of this book may be used or reproduced in any manner for the purpose of training artificial intelligence technologies or systems.

MAD LIBS and logo are registered trademarks of Penguin Random House LLC.

Visit us online at penguinrandomhouse.com.

Manufactured in China

ISBN 9780593889947

1 3 5 7 9 10 8 6 4 2

HH

The authorized representative in the EU for product safety and compliance is Penguin Random House Ireland, Morrison Chambers, 32 Nassau Street, Dublin D02 YH68, Ireland, https://eu-contact.penguin.ie.

MAD LIBS®
INSTRUCTIONS

MAD LIBS® is a game for people who don't like games! It can be played by one, two, three, four, or forty.

• RIDICULOUSLY SIMPLE DIRECTIONS

In this tablet you will find stories containing blank spaces where words are left out. One player, the READER, selects one of these stories. The READER does not tell anyone what the story is about. Instead, he/she asks the other players, the WRITERS, to give him/her words. These words are used to fill in the blank spaces in the story.

• TO PLAY

The READER asks each WRITER in turn to call out a word—an adjective or a noun or whatever the space calls for—and uses them to fill in the blank spaces in the story. The result is a MAD LIBS® game.

When the READER then reads the completed MAD LIBS® game to the other players, they will discover that they have written a story that is fantastic, screamingly funny, shocking, silly, crazy, or just plain dumb—depending upon which words each WRITER called out.

• EXAMPLE (*Before* and *After*)

"_____!" he said _____
       EXCLAMATION   ADVERB

as he jumped into his convertible _____ and
                                            NOUN

drove off with his _____ wife.
                         ADJECTIVE

"_____OUCH_____!" he said _____HAPPILY_____
       EXCLAMATION   ADVERB

as he jumped into his convertible _____CAT_____ and
                                            NOUN

drove off with his _____BRAVE_____ wife.
                         ADJECTIVE

MAD LIBS
QUICK REVIEW

In case you have forgotten what adjectives, adverbs, nouns, and verbs are, here is a quick review:

An ADJECTIVE describes something or somebody. *Lumpy*, *soft*, *ugly*, *messy*, and *short* are adjectives.

An ADVERB tells how something is done. It modifies a verb and usually ends in "ly." *Modestly*, *stupidly*, *greedily*, and *carefully* are adverbs.

A NOUN is the name of a person, place, or thing. *Sidewalk*, *umbrella*, *bridle*, *bathtub*, and *nose* are nouns.

A VERB is an action word. *Run*, *pitch*, *jump*, and *swim* are verbs. Put the verbs in past tense if the directions say PAST TENSE. *Ran*, *pitched*, *jumped*, and *swam* are verbs in the past tense.

When we ask for A PLACE, we mean any sort of place: a country or city (*Spain*, *Cleveland*) or a room (*bathroom*, *kitchen*).

An EXCLAMATION or SILLY WORD is any sort of funny sound, gasp, grunt, or outcry, like *Wow!*, *Ouch!*, *Whomp!*, *Ick!*, and *Gadzooks!*

When we ask for specific words, like a NUMBER, a COLOR, an ANIMAL, or a PART OF THE BODY, we mean a word that is one of those things, like *seven*, *blue*, *horse*, or *head*.

When we ask for a PLURAL, it means more than one. For example, *cat* pluralized is *cats*.

WHAT I'M THANKFUL FOR

ADJECTIVE _____

PERSON YOU KNOW _____

PLURAL NOUN _____

NOUN _____

NOUN _____

PART OF THE BODY _____

PLURAL NOUN _____

TYPE OF LIQUID _____

PART OF THE BODY _____

ANIMAL _____

ADJECTIVE _____

NOUN _____

PLURAL NOUN _____

PLURAL NOUN _____

NUMBER _____

SOMETHING ALIVE _____

MAD LIBS® is fun to play with friends, but you can also play it by yourself! To begin with, DO NOT look at the story on the page below. Fill in the blanks on this page with the words called for. Then, using the words you have selected, fill in the blank spaces in the story.

Now you've created your own hilarious MAD LIBS® game!

WHAT I'M THANKFUL FOR

This Thanksgiving, I'm thankful for all the _____ things in
ADJECTIVE

my life. Even though I complain about how _____ is always
PERSON YOU KNOW

getting on my nerves, or how studying _____ is boring, or
PLURAL NOUN

how I hate cleaning my _____, I know I am a very lucky
NOUN

_____. I have a roof over my _____. I always have
NOUN PART OF THE BODY

enough _____ to eat and _____ to drink. I have
PLURAL NOUNTYPE OF LIQUID

a good _____ on my shoulders, and I am as healthy as a/an
PART OF THE BODY

_____. My _____ family loves me, even when I act
ANIMAL ADJECTIVE

like a/an _____. And my friends always have my best
NOUN

_____ at heart. Yep, I've got all the _____
PLURAL NOUN PLURAL NOUN

I need, and now I get to eat a/an _____-course Thanksgiving
NUMBER

meal, too. What more could a/an _____ ask for?
SOMETHING ALIVE

From TURKEY TIME MAD LIBS® • Copyright © 2013, 2025 by PENGUIN RANDOM HOUSE LLC

WHAT'S FOR DINNER?

TYPE OF FOOD _____

PERSON YOU KNOW _____

VERB _____

PART OF THE BODY (PLURAL) _____

ADJECTIVE _____

NOUN _____

NOUN _____

PLURAL NOUN _____

TYPE OF LIQUID _____

ADJECTIVE _____

NOUN _____

NOUN _____

TYPE OF FOOD _____

TYPE OF FOOD (PLURAL) _____

PERSON YOU KNOW (FEMALE) _____

NOUN _____

PART OF THE BODY (PLURAL) _____

MAD LIBS® is fun to play with friends, but you can also play it by yourself! To begin with, DO NOT look at the story on the page below. Fill in the blanks on this page with the words called for. Then, using the words you have selected, fill in the blank spaces in the story.

Now you've created your own hilarious MAD LIBS® game!

WHAT'S FOR DINNER?

It was Thanksgiving, and the scent of succulent roast _____
                                                       TYPE OF FOOD
wafted through my house. "_____, it's time to
                              PERSON YOU KNOW
_____!" my mother called. I couldn't wait to get my
     VERB
_____ on that _____ Thanksgiving meal.
PART OF THE BODY (PLURAL)   ADJECTIVE
My family sat around the dining-room _____. The table was
                                          NOUN
laid out with every kind of _____ imaginable. There was
                                   NOUN
a basket of hot buttered _____ and glasses of sparkling
                            PLURAL NOUN
_____. The _____ turkey sat, steaming, next to a
TYPE OF LIQUID   ADJECTIVE
bowl of _____ gravy. A bowl of ruby-red _____
          NOUN   NOUN
sauce, a sweet-_____ casserole, and a dish of mashed
                  TYPE OF FOOD
_____ tempted my taste buds. But the dish I looked
TYPE OF FOOD (PLURAL)
forward to most was Grandma _____'s famous
                              PERSON YOU KNOW (FEMALE)
_____ pie. Thanksgiving is my favorite holiday,
         NOUN
_____ down.
PART OF THE BODY (PLURAL)

From TURKEY TIME MAD LIBS® • Copyright © 2013, 2025 by Penguin Random House LLC

MAD LIBS® is fun to play with friends, but you can also play it by yourself! To begin with, DO NOT look at the story on the page below. Fill in the blanks on this page with the words called for. Then, using the words you have selected, fill in the blank spaces in the story.

Now you've created your own hilarious MAD LIBS® game!

BALLOON GOES BUST

ADJECTIVE _____

A PLACE _____

NOUN _____

A PLACE _____

VERB ENDING IN "ING" _____

ADJECTIVE _____

EXCLAMATION _____

NOUN _____

PART OF THE BODY _____

ADJECTIVE _____

PART OF THE BODY (PLURAL) _____

PART OF THE BODY _____

PLURAL NOUN _____

PART OF THE BODY (PLURAL) _____

VERB ENDING IN "ING" _____

BALLOON GOES BUST

This story is to be read aloud by two _____ narrators.
                                        ADJECTIVE

TV Announcer #1: Welcome, one and all, to the thirty-third annual

_____ Thanksgiving parade.
  A PLACE

TV Announcer #2: These floats are a/an _____ to behold.
                                              NOUN

Look! The famous _____ turkey balloon is _____
                  A PLACE   VERB ENDING IN "ING"

our way!

TV Announcer #1: Oh no! The balloon is caught on a/an _____
                                                            ADJECTIVE

traffic light!

TV Announcer #2: _____! It appears a/an _____
                      EXCLAMATION   NOUN

has pierced the balloon's _____! The turkey is losing
                            PART OF THE BODY

air at a/an _____ rate!
              ADJECTIVE

TV Announcer #1: Children along the parade route are crying their

_____ out. This is not a sight for the faint of
PART OF THE BODY (PLURAL)

_____, folks.
PART OF THE BODY

TV Announcer #2: TV viewers, if you have small _____
                                                      PLURAL NOUN

at home, please cover their _____! It's a
                              PART OF THE BODY (PLURAL)

Thanks-_____ disaster!
         VERB ENDING IN "ING"

From TURKEY TIME MAD LIBS® • Copyright © 2013, 2025 by Penguin Random House LLC

MAD LIBS® is fun to play with friends, but you can also play it by yourself! To begin with, DO NOT look at the story on the page below. Fill in the blanks on this page with the words called for. Then, using the words you have selected, fill in the blank spaces in the story.

Now you've created your own hilarious MAD LIBS® game!

HOW TO ROAST A TURKEY

_____ PART OF THE BODY
_____ NUMBER
_____ TYPE OF LIQUID
_____ PLURAL NOUN
_____ PLURAL NOUN
_____ PLURAL NOUN
_____ TYPE OF FOOD
_____ NOUN
_____ ADVERB
_____ PART OF THE BODY
_____ TYPE OF FOOD
_____ TYPE OF LIQUID
_____ PART OF THE BODY
_____ PART OF THE BODY
_____ NUMBER
_____ ADJECTIVE
_____ ADVERB

HOW TO ROAST A TURKEY

To roast a turkey, you first have to remove the turkey's neck, heart, gizzard, and _____. Then preheat the oven to _____
                     PART OF THE BODY   NUMBER

degrees. Wash out the turkey with _____, then fill it with
                                      TYPE OF LIQUID

stuffing. Popular stuffing ingredients include cubed _____,
                                                                     PLURAL NOUN

celery, raisins, onion, and _____. Close up the turkey
                                 PLURAL NOUN

cavity using string or metal _____. Rub melted
                                      PLURAL NOUN

_____ or _____ oil all over the outside of the turkey,
TYPE OF FOOD   NOUN

then sprinkle it _____ with salt and pepper. Place the whole
                    ADVERB

thing, _____ down, in a pan, and add several sprigs of fresh
      PART OF THE BODY

_____. Put it in the oven with a tray beneath it to catch any
TYPE OF FOOD

_____ that might drip from the turkey's _____.
TYPE OF LIQUID   PART OF THE BODY

Every half hour, stick a thermometer into the turkey's _____
                                                                                       PART OF THE BODY

to make sure it doesn't rise above _____ degrees. The turkey is
                                                      NUMBER

done when its juices appear _____. Take the turkey out of the
                                  ADJECTIVE

oven, carve _____, and enjoy!
            ADVERB

From TURKEY TIME MAD LIBS® • Copyright © 2013, 2025 by Penguin Random House LLC

FOOTBALL FIASCO

PLURAL NOUN _____

A PLACE _____

ANIMAL (PLURAL) _____

NUMBER _____

SAME NUMBER _____

NOUN _____

ADJECTIVE _____

ADVERB _____

NUMBER _____

VERB (PAST TENSE) _____

ADJECTIVE _____

SAME ADJECTIVE _____

VERB ENDING IN "ING" _____

PART OF THE BODY _____

ADVERB _____

VERB (PAST TENSE) _____

ADVERB _____

MAD LIBS® is fun to play with friends, but you can also play it by yourself! To begin with, DO NOT look at the story on the page below. Fill in the blanks on this page with the words called for. Then, using the words you have selected, fill in the blank spaces in the story.

Now you've created your own hilarious MAD LIBS® game!

FOOTBALL FIASCO

It was the fourth quarter in the big Thanksgiving Day game between the Detroit _____ and the _____
PLURAL NOUN   A PLACE

_____. The score was tied _____–
ANIMAL (PLURAL)   NUMBER

_____, and you could feel the tension throughout
SAME NUMBER

the huge _____ Stadium. With only five minutes left,
NOUN

Detroit had just called a time-out when, suddenly, fans noticed a/an

_____ commotion down on the field. A turkey had somehow
ADJECTIVE

gotten loose and was running _____ across the
ADVERB

_____-yard line! The crowd _____ with laughter
NUMBER   VERB (PAST TENSE)

as the referees chased the _____ bird. Members of both teams
ADJECTIVE

joined the refs in chasing the _____ turkey, which tried to
SAME ADJECTIVE

outrun the Detroit _____ back who eventually caught
VERB ENDING IN "ING"

him by the _____. After that, the tension throughout the
PART OF THE BODY

stadium _____ broken, the fans hardly cared who won or
ADVERB

_____. The runaway turkey had _____ stolen
VERB (PAST TENSE)   ADVERB

the show!

From TURKEY TIME MAD LIBS® • Copyright © 2013, 2025 by Penguin Random House LLC

MAD LIBS® is fun to play with friends, but you can also play it by yourself! To begin with, DO NOT look at the story on the page below. Fill in the blanks on this page with the words called for. Then, using the words you have selected, fill in the blank spaces in the story.

Now you've created your own hilarious MAD LIBS® game!

THE FIRST THANKSGIVING

_____ NUMBER
_____ A PLACE
_____ NOUN
_____ ADJECTIVE
_____ SOMETHING ALIVE (PLURAL)
_____ VERB
_____ TYPE OF FOOD (PLURAL)
_____ PLURAL NOUN
_____ ADJECTIVE
_____ ADJECTIVE
_____ NUMBER
_____ PLURAL NOUN
_____ ADJECTIVE
_____ NOUN
_____ ADVERB
_____ PLURAL NOUN
_____ ADJECTIVE

THE FIRST THANKSGIVING

In late 1620, _____ Pilgrims arrived at Plymouth Rock. They
           NUMBER

had come all the way from (the) _____ to find religious
                                  A PLACE

freedom in America. But life in the New _____ was not
                                              NOUN

easy. Their first winter was _____, and many
                                   ADJECTIVE

_____ fell ill. Luckily, the following year, Native
SOMETHING ALIVE (PLURAL)

Americans taught the Pilgrims how to _____ crops like corn
                                          VERB

and _____. By that November, the Pilgrims had
      TYPE OF FOOD (PLURAL)

plenty of _____ to harvest, so they decided to have a/an
             PLURAL NOUN

_____ feast. Some Native American friends joined the
     ADJECTIVE

_____ Pilgrims, and the festival lasted for _____
    ADJECTIVE   NUMBER

days. They ate the _____ of their harvest as well as
                         PLURAL NOUN

deer and several _____ birds. It was a/an _____
                    ADJECTIVE   NOUN

to remember, and has since become known as the first Thanksgiving.

While the menu has changed _____ over the years,
                                  ADVERB

Thanksgiving is still a time to celebrate our _____ and
                                                  PLURAL NOUN

our _____ fortune.
         ADJECTIVE

From TURKEY TIME MAD LIBS® • Copyright © 2013, 2025 by Penguin Random House LLC

TRAVEL DISASTER

ADJECTIVE _____
ADJECTIVE _____
A PLACE _____
PERSON YOU KNOW (FEMALE) _____
PERSON YOU KNOW (MALE) _____
NOUN _____
NOUN _____
VERB (PAST TENSE) _____
NUMBER _____
VEHICLE _____
NOUN _____
ADJECTIVE _____
ADJECTIVE _____
ADJECTIVE _____
ADVERB _____
TYPE OF LIQUID _____
NOUN _____

MAD LIBS® is fun to play with friends, but you can also play it by yourself! To begin with, DO NOT look at the story on the page below. Fill in the blanks on this page with the words called for. Then, using the words you have selected, fill in the blank spaces in the story.

Now you've created your own hilarious MAD LIBS® game!

TRAVEL DISASTER

Flying for Thanksgiving is always a/an _____ nightmare,
                                          ADJECTIVE

but this year was particularly _____. My family was
                                       ADJECTIVE

supposed to go to (the) boring old _____ to visit my aunt
                                          A PLACE

_____ and uncle _____. But
   PERSON YOU KNOW (FEMALE)   PERSON YOU KNOW (MALE)

when we got to the airport, a/an _____ storm delayed our
                                          NOUN

flight. After we boarded the _____, we _____
                                     NOUN   VERB (PAST TENSE)

on the runway for _____ hours because of a mechanical difficulty.
                      NUMBER

They eventually drove us back to the gate and rescheduled us on a new

_____. When we finally took off, the pilot said, "Welcome
   VEHICLE

aboard _____ Airlines. Enjoy your _____ flight to
               NOUN   ADJECTIVE

Hawaii." *Hawaii?!* We were on the wrong plane! But we embraced the

_____ mess-up. Hawaii was a far more _____
        ADJECTIVE   ADJECTIVE

destination than our aunt and uncle's! We laughed _____ the
                                                          ADVERB

whole flight there and enjoyed frozen coconut _____ on the
                                                      TYPE OF LIQUID

beach for our Thanksgiving dinner. It was a/an _____ to
                                                         NOUN

remember!

MAD LIBS® is fun to play with friends, but you can also play it by yourself! To begin with, DO NOT look at the story on the page below. Fill in the blanks on this page with the words called for. Then, using the words you have selected, fill in the blank spaces in the story.

Now you've created your own hilarious MAD LIBS® game!

HOW THANKSGIVING BECAME A HOLIDAY

_____ ADJECTIVE

_____ OCCUPATION (PLURAL)

_____ ADJECTIVE

_____ A PLACE

_____ VERB

_____ ADJECTIVE

_____ SOMETHING ALIVE (PLURAL)

_____ PLURAL NOUN

_____ ADJECTIVE

_____ ADJECTIVE

_____ PERSON YOU KNOW

_____ ADJECTIVE

_____ SAME SOMETHING ALIVE (PLURAL)

TURKEY TIME MAD LIBS

HOW THANKSGIVING BECAME A HOLIDAY

Even though the first Thanksgiving took place in 1621, Thanksgiving didn't become a national holiday until a/an _____
ADJECTIVE
woman named Sarah Josepha Hale came along. In the 1800s, Ms. Hale was one of the first female _____ at a/an _____
OCCUPATION (PLURAL)   ADJECTIVE
magazine. She was famous throughout (the) _____
A PLACE
for her articles encouraging women to _____, exercise,
VERB
and get a/an _____ education. But one of Sarah's
ADJECTIVE
biggest ideas was to make Thanksgiving a national holiday, to be celebrated by _____ across America. At the
SOMETHING ALIVE (PLURAL)
time, Thanksgiving was only celebrated by a few _____.
PLURAL NOUN
Sarah wrote _____ letters to one president after another,
ADJECTIVE
trying to convince them of how _____ Thanksgiving was. No
ADJECTIVE
one listened—at least not until President _____. They
PERSON YOU KNOW
declared Thanksgiving a/an _____ holiday in
ADJECTIVE
1863, and _____ around the country have
SAME SOMETHING ALIVE (PLURAL)
been celebrating it ever since.

From TURKEY TIME MAD LIBS® • Copyright © 2013, 2025 by Penguin Random House LLC

LIFE'S A MAIZE

ADJECTIVE _____

NOUN _____

ADJECTIVE _____

NOUN _____

TYPE OF FOOD _____

VERB ENDING IN "ING" _____

NOUN _____

PLURAL NOUN _____

PLURAL NOUN _____

NOUN _____

VEHICLE (PLURAL) _____

PLURAL NOUN _____

ADJECTIVE _____

PLURAL NOUN _____

ARTICLE OF CLOTHING _____

NOUN _____

PLURAL NOUN _____

NOUN _____

MAD LIBS® is fun to play with friends, but you can also play it by yourself! To begin with, DO NOT look at the story on the page below. Fill in the blanks on this page with the words called for. Then, using the words you have selected, fill in the blank spaces in the story.

Now you've created your own hilarious MAD LIBS® game!

LIFE'S A MAIZE

Corn is a/an _____ staple of the autumn harvest, and it can be
                ADJECTIVE

found on many a Thanksgiving _____. But corn has many
                                    NOUN

other _____ uses, too! Corn can be found in:
        ADJECTIVE

Food products: Aside from corn on the _____, you can find
                                                NOUN

corn in _____ butter, _____ gum, and
         TYPE OF FOOD   VERB ENDING IN "ING"

_____ -flavored sodas.
    NOUN

Plastics: Plastics made from corn _____ are more popular
                                        PLURAL NOUN

than ever before. You can often recycle plastic _____ made
                                                  PLURAL NOUN

from corn, too!

Fuel: Ethanol is a popular corn _____ used to fuel cars,
                                        NOUN

_____, and even rocket _____.
VEHICLE (PLURAL)   PLURAL NOUN

Household products: Manufacturers often use corn to help make

_____ soaps, scented _____, _____
  ADJECTIVE   PLURAL NOUN   ARTICLE OF CLOTHING

polish, and even _____ batteries!
                    NOUN

Everywhere you look, corn _____ can be found. It's not
                            PLURAL NOUN

just a super food, it's a super _____, too!
                                    NOUN

From TURKEY TIME MAD LIBS® • Copyright © 2013, 2025 by Penguin Random House LLC

MAD LIBS® is fun to play with friends, but you can also play it by yourself! To begin with, DO NOT look at the story on the page below. Fill in the blanks on this page with the words called for. Then, using the words you have selected, fill in the blank spaces in the story.

Now you've created your own hilarious MAD LIBS® game!

STUFFING YOURSELF SILLY

_____ TYPE OF EVENT
_____ TYPE OF FOOD (PLURAL)
_____ ADJECTIVE
_____ PLURAL NOUN
_____ PLURAL NOUN
_____ PLURAL NOUN
_____ VERB (PAST TENSE)
_____ NOUN
_____ ADJECTIVE
_____ SILLY WORD
_____ SAME SILLY WORD
_____ PLURAL NOUN
_____ PART OF THE BODY
_____ OCCUPATION (PLURAL)
_____ NOUN
_____ TYPE OF FOOD

STUFFING YOURSELF SILLY

Thanksgiving is not a/an _____ to be taken lightly. In order
                                TYPE OF EVENT
to eat as many _____ as possible, you need to have
                  TYPE OF FOOD (PLURAL)
a/an _____ strategy. Follow these handy-dandy _____,
       ADJECTIVE   PLURAL NOUN
and you, too, can own Thanksgiving.

Tip #1: Load up on the most popular _____ first.
                                            PLURAL NOUN
Mashed _____ and gravy tend to be the first to go,
          PLURAL NOUN
and _____ sweet potatoes and cranberry _____
     VERB (PAST TENSE)   NOUN
go fast, too. Get 'em while they're _____!
                                       ADJECTIVE

Tip #2: Stick with light meat. Dark meat contains more _____
                                                              SILLY WORD
than light meat, and everyone knows that _____ makes
                                            SAME SILLY WORD
you sleepy when you eat it. If you're sleeping, you won't be able to eat
_____!
    PLURAL NOUN

Tip #3: Don't worry about saving room in your _____ for
                                                     PART OF THE BODY
dessert. Studies by famous _____ show that no matter
                              OCCUPATION (PLURAL)
how much _____ you've eaten, you always have room for
            NOUN
dessert—especially if it's _____ pie!
                              TYPE OF FOOD

From TURKEY TIME MAD LIBS® • Copyright © 2013, 2025 by Penguin Random House LLC

CANADIAN THANKSGIVING

_____ NUMBER
_____ A PLACE
_____ PERSON IN ROOM
_____ ADJECTIVE
_____ ADJECTIVE
_____ NOUN
_____ ADJECTIVE
_____ PLURAL NOUN
_____ TYPE OF FOOD (PLURAL)
_____ NOUN
_____ VERB
_____ PLURAL NOUN
_____ ADJECTIVE

MAD LIBS® is fun to play with friends, but you can also play it by yourself! To begin with, DO NOT look at the story on the page below. Fill in the blanks on this page with the words called for. Then, using the words you have selected, fill in the blank spaces in the story.

Now you've created your own hilarious MAD LIBS® game!

CANADIAN THANKSGIVING

Did you know that the first Thanksgiving in North America was actually in Canada, _____ years before the Pilgrims arrived in
NUMBER
(the) _____? The first Canadian Thanksgiving took place in
A PLACE
1578, when explorer _____ arrived in Newfoundland
PERSON IN ROOM
and wanted to give thanks for their _____ arrival
ADJECTIVE
in the _____ World. Beginning in 1957, Canadian
ADJECTIVE
Parliament declared that the second Monday in October would be a day to celebrate "the bountiful _____ with which Canada has
NOUN
been blessed." Today, Canadians still celebrate their own _____
ADJECTIVE
_____-giving, which is similar to American Thanksgiving in
PLURAL NOUN
many ways. Canadians eat turkey and _____, and
TYPE OF FOOD (PLURAL)
they watch Canadian _____-ball, too! Most importantly,
NOUN
Canadians _____ thanks for all of their _____.
VERB   PLURAL NOUN
And what's more _____ than that, eh?
ADJECTIVE

From TURKEY TIME MAD LIBS® • Copyright © 2013, 2025 by Penguin Random House LLC

MAD LIBS® is fun to play with friends, but you can also play it by yourself! To begin with, DO NOT look at the story on the page below. Fill in the blanks on this page with the words called for. Then, using the words you have selected, fill in the blank spaces in the story.

Now you've created your own hilarious MAD LIBS® game!

A THANKSGIVING SPECIAL

_____ A PLACE
_____ ADJECTIVE
_____ VERB (PAST TENSE)
_____ ANIMAL
_____ EXCLAMATION
_____ NOUN
_____ SAME ANIMAL
_____ ADJECTIVE
_____ PERSON YOU KNOW
_____ OCCUPATION
_____ ADJECTIVE
_____ ADJECTIVE
_____ SOMETHING ALIVE (PLURAL)
_____ PLURAL NOUN
_____ SAME OCCUPATION
_____ SOMETHING ALIVE
_____ PLURAL NOUN

A THANKSGIVING SPECIAL

It was Thanksgiving, and all the people in (the) _____
                                                   A PLACE
were ready for their annual Thanksgiving celebration. There was just
one problem: The _____ turkey was missing! The townspeople
                    ADJECTIVE
_____ high and low, but the _____ was
    VERB (PAST TENSE)   ANIMAL
nowhere to be found. "_____!" little Sally _____
                         EXCLAMATION   NOUN
said. "We can't have Thanksgiving without a/an _____!"
                                                  SAME ANIMAL
Just then, a/an _____ figure appeared. It was
                         ADJECTIVE
_____, the mean old _____ who lived on
  PERSON YOU KNOW   OCCUPATION
top of a/an _____ hill and never came to visit. "I took your
              ADJECTIVE
_____ turkey!" they shouted. "You _____
  ADJECTIVE   SOMETHING ALIVE (PLURAL)
are so thankful, but what do you have to be thankful for?" "We have
our friends, our families, and our _____!" said little
                                        PLURAL NOUN
Sally. "Just because *you* don't have any doesn't mean you should ruin
our Thanksgiving, you mean old _____!" The
                                      SAME OCCUPATION
townspeople cheered, and the grumpy _____ saw the
                                          SOMETHING ALIVE
error of their ways. They returned the town turkey and joined in the
celebration. "Happy Thanksgiving to _____ everywhere!"
                                        PLURAL NOUN
little Sally cheered.

From TURKEY TIME MAD LIBS® • Copyright © 2013, 2025 by Penguin Random House LLC

MAD LIBS® is fun to play with friends, but you can also play it by yourself! To begin with, DO NOT look at the story on the page below. Fill in the blanks on this page with the words called for. Then, using the words you have selected, fill in the blank spaces in the story.

Now you've created your own hilarious MAD LIBS® game!

PILGRIM KID

_____ ADJECTIVE

_____ TYPE OF FOOD (PLURAL)

_____ ARTICLE OF CLOTHING

_____ PART OF THE BODY

_____ PLURAL NOUN

_____ NOUN

_____ PERSON YOU KNOW (MALE)

_____ PERSON YOU KNOW (FEMALE)

_____ ADJECTIVE

_____ ADJECTIVE

_____ ADVERB

_____ PART OF THE BODY (PLURAL)

_____ NOUN

_____ VERB (PAST TENSE)

PILGRIM KID

Dear Ye Olde Diary,

Life as a wee Pilgrim child is more _____ by the day. Today,
                                      ADJECTIVE

Mother sent me to the garden to pick some fresh _____
                                                 TYPE OF FOOD (PLURAL)

for supper. The sun was hot, and I was wearing my black-and-white

_____, which did not keep my _____ cool.
ARTICLE OF CLOTHING   PART OF THE BODY

Afterward, Father insisted that I help him catch _____
                                                  PLURAL NOUN

for dinner, but we only found one small _____.
                                          NOUN

Alas! While Mother and Father cooked, I went to play with my brother

_____ and sister _____,
PERSON YOU KNOW (MALE)   PERSON YOU KNOW (FEMALE)

but we hath only one toy—a/an _____ rock. Our
                                ADJECTIVE

_____ game of Kick the Rock soon became _____
ADJECTIVE   ADVERB

tiresome. Nay, we were bored out of our _____!
                                          PART OF THE BODY (PLURAL)

Aye, life as a Pilgrim _____ is not all it's _____
                        NOUN   VERB (PAST TENSE)

up to be!

From TURKEY TIME MAD LIBS® • Copyright © 2013, 2025 by Penguin Random House LLC

THE LAST TURKEY

TYPE OF FOOD _____
A PLACE _____
ADJECTIVE _____
ANIMAL _____
ADJECTIVE _____
PERSON YOU KNOW _____
SOMETHING ALIVE _____
PART OF THE BODY (PLURAL) _____
PLURAL NOUN _____
PLURAL NOUN _____
VERB ENDING IN "ING" _____
VERB ENDING IN "ING" _____
SAME VERB ENDING IN "ING" _____
PERSON YOU KNOW (FEMALE) _____
ADJECTIVE _____
ADJECTIVE _____
ADJECTIVE _____

MAD LIBS® is fun to play with friends, but you can also play it by yourself! To begin with, DO NOT look at the story on the page below. Fill in the blanks on this page with the words called for. Then, using the words you have selected, fill in the blank spaces in the story.

Now you've created your own hilarious MAD LIBS® game!

THE LAST TURKEY

It was Thanksgiving, and our family didn't have a/an _____ to
                                                    TYPE OF FOOD
roast. We hopped in the car and drove to (the) _____, but they
                                                   A PLACE
were all out of _____ turkeys. "We have ham and duck and
                   ADJECTIVE
_____, though!" said the man at the deli counter. "It's not
   ANIMAL
Thanksgiving without a/an _____ turkey!" my dad replied.
                              ADJECTIVE
So we got back in the car and drove to _____'s Grocery.
                                          PERSON YOU KNOW
They had one turkey left—but another _____ grabbed the
                                        SOMETHING ALIVE
turkey before we could get our _____ on it. "Come
                                  PART OF THE BODY (PLURAL)
on, _____," said my mom. "Let's just go out for Chinese
      PLURAL NOUN
_____ instead." But on the drive to the restaurant, we
   PLURAL NOUN
spotted a wild turkey _____ across the road. "Are you
                         VERB ENDING IN "ING"
_____ what I'm _____?" my sister
  VERB ENDING IN "ING"   SAME VERB (ENDING IN "ING")
_____ said. We all got out of the car and
  PERSON YOU KNOW (FEMALE)
chased the _____ bird down the road. But once we got
               ADJECTIVE
the _____ turkey home, we couldn't bear to eat him—so we
      ADJECTIVE
made him our _____ family pet instead!
                ADJECTIVE

From TURKEY TIME MAD LIBS® • Copyright © 2013, 2025 by Penguin Random House LLC

MAD LIBS® is fun to play with friends, but you can also play it by yourself! To begin with, DO NOT look at the story on the page below. Fill in the blanks on this page with the words called for. Then, using the words you have selected, fill in the blank spaces in the story.

Now you've created your own hilarious MAD LIBS® game!

TABLE TALK

_____ SOMETHING ALIVE
_____ VERB ENDING IN "ING"
_____ VERB
_____ PLURAL NOUN
_____ NUMBER
_____ TYPE OF LIQUID
_____ TYPE OF FOOD
_____ VEHICLE
_____ TYPE OF LIQUID
_____ ADJECTIVE
_____ PLURAL NOUN
_____ ANIMAL (PLURAL)
_____ SOMETHING ALIVE (PLURAL)
_____ VERB
_____ PERSON YOU KNOW
_____ CELEBRITY
_____ VERB ENDING IN "ING"

TABLE TALK

Are you the lucky _____ in charge of _____
                   SOMETHING ALIVE   VERB ENDING IN "ING"

the Thanksgiving table? Here are some helpful tips:

1. Forks always _____ to the left of dinner plates, while
                    VERB

   _____ go to the right.
   PLURAL NOUN

2. Set out _____ glasses for each guest, so they can sip both
              NUMBER

   water and _____.
              TYPE OF LIQUID

3. Don't forget small _____ plates, as well as a gravy
                         TYPE OF FOOD

   _____ for pouring the all-important _____.
   VEHICLE   TYPE OF LIQUID

4. If you're feeling _____, fold napkins in the shape
                        ADJECTIVE

   of _____ or adorable _____! Create a
      PLURAL NOUN   ANIMAL (PLURAL)

   festive centerpiece with a bouquet of _____.
                                          SOMETHING ALIVE (PLURAL)

5. Set place cards so everyone knows exactly where to _____.
                                                       VERB

   But be careful, you don't want _____ sitting next to
                                    PERSON YOU KNOW

   your aunt _____ or they might get into a heated debate
              CELEBRITY

   about the dangers of global _____!
                                VERB ENDING IN "ING"

From TURKEY TIME MAD LIBS® • Copyright © 2013, 2025 by Penguin Random House LLC

MAD LIBS® is fun to play with friends, but you can also play it by yourself! To begin with, DO NOT look at the story on the page below. Fill in the blanks on this page with the words called for. Then, using the words you have selected, fill in the blank spaces in the story.

Now you've created your own hilarious MAD LIBS® game!

THANKSGIVING FACTS

_____ SOMETHING ALIVE (PLURAL)
_____ TYPE OF FOOD (PLURAL)
_____ NUMBER
_____ ADJECTIVE
_____ NOUN
_____ NOUN
_____ TYPE OF FOOD
_____ TYPE OF FOOD (PLURAL)
_____ ANIMAL (PLURAL)
_____ PLURAL NOUN
_____ ANIMAL (PLURAL)
_____ PLURAL NOUN
_____ VERB (PAST TENSE)
_____ PLURAL NOUN
_____ PLURAL NOUN

THANKSGIVING FACTS

- Each Thanksgiving, _____ in the United States
  SOMETHING ALIVE (PLURAL)
  consume forty-six million _____. That's almost
  TYPE OF FOOD (PLURAL)
  _____ pounds of turkey per person!
  NUMBER

- _____ inventor and politician Benjamin Franklin
  ADJECTIVE
  described the turkey as a/an "_____ of Courage."
  NOUN

- TV dinners originated when a company called _____ had
  NOUN
  too much leftover frozen _____ after Thanksgiving; they
  TYPE OF FOOD
  began packaging the turkey with potatoes, _____,
  TYPE OF FOOD (PLURAL)
  and other foods into the first frozen meals.

- The tradition of Thanksgiving football began when the owner of
  the Detroit _____ wanted to build up the team's
  ANIMAL (PLURAL)
  loyal _____. On Thanksgiving Day 1934, they played
  PLURAL NOUN
  the Chicago _____ and lost.
  ANIMAL (PLURAL)

- According to *Guinness World* _____, the largest
  PLURAL NOUN
  pumpkin pie ever _____ weighed three thousand
  VERB (PAST TENSE)
  seven hundred _____ and measured twenty
  PLURAL NOUN
  _____ across.
  PLURAL NOUN

From TURKEY TIME MAD LIBS® • Copyright © 2013, 2025 by Penguin Random House LLC

MAD LIBS® is fun to play with friends, but you can also play it by yourself! To begin with, DO NOT look at the story on the page below. Fill in the blanks on this page with the words called for. Then, using the words you have selected, fill in the blank spaces in the story.

Now you've created your own hilarious MAD LIBS® game!

PARDON THAT TURKEY

PLURAL NOUN _____

ADJECTIVE _____

SOMETHING ALIVE (PLURAL) _____

ADJECTIVE _____

NOUN _____

COLOR _____

PLURAL NOUN _____

A PLACE _____

ADJECTIVE _____

VERB _____

ADJECTIVE _____

PERSON IN ROOM _____

ADJECTIVE _____

OCCUPATION _____

VERB (PAST TENSE) _____

PARDON THAT TURKEY

Each year, the president of the United _____ is presented
                                            PLURAL NOUN
with two _____ turkeys to pardon. That means the
          ADJECTIVE
president spares them from being eaten by _____
                                             SOMETHING ALIVE (PLURAL)
on Thanksgiving. The president formally pardons the _____
                                                        ADJECTIVE
birds in the _____ Garden of the _____ House,
              NOUN   COLOR
while television _____ and families from all over (the)
                   PLURAL NOUN
_____ witness the _____ spectacle. The pardoned
 A PLACE   ADJECTIVE
turkeys get to _____ out the rest of their days on a/an
                 VERB
_____ farm at President _____'s estate, Mount
 ADJECTIVE   PERSON IN ROOM
Vernon. To this day, twenty-two _____ turkeys have been
                                    ADJECTIVE
pardoned by the _____. To those turkeys, it must feel like
                   OCCUPATION
they've _____ the lottery!
          VERB (PAST TENSE)

From TURKEY TIME MAD LIBS® • Copyright © 2013, 2025 by Penguin Random House LLC

MAD LIBS® is fun to play with friends, but you can also play it by yourself! To begin with, DO NOT look at the story on the page below. Fill in the blanks on this page with the words called for. Then, using the words you have selected, fill in the blank spaces in the story.

Now you've created your own hilarious MAD LIBS® game!

PICK YOUR PIE

_____ VERB ENDING IN "ING"
_____ NOUN
_____ ADJECTIVE
_____ NUMBER
_____ TYPE OF FOOD (PLURAL)
_____ ADJECTIVE
_____ ADJECTIVE
_____ VERB
_____ ADJECTIVE
_____ ADJECTIVE
_____ ADJECTIVE
_____ TYPE OF FOOD
_____ ADJECTIVE
_____ NOUN

PICK YOUR PIE

Do you love _____ pie on Thanksgiving? Who doesn't?
              VERB ENDING IN "ING"

The only problem is choosing which _____ to eat! Take this
                                         NOUN

quiz to find out your _____ preference!
                         ADJECTIVE

1. Your favorite kind of pie involves (a) _____ slices of fruit, (b)
                                              NUMBER

   nuts and _____, or (c) _____ vegetables.
            TYPE OF FOOD (PLURAL)   ADJECTIVE

2. Of these three _____ options, your favorite color of food
                     ADJECTIVE

   to _____ is (a) yellow, (b) brown, or (c) orange.
        VERB

3. Do you prefer your food to be (a) gooey and sweet with a touch of

   _____ cinnamon, (b) sweet with a sprinkling of
         ADJECTIVE

   _____ salt, or (c) mushy and _____?
     ADJECTIVE   ADJECTIVE

If you picked mostly *a*'s, apple _____ is your favorite
                                       TYPE OF FOOD

Thanksgiving treat. If you picked mostly *b*'s, you are a big fan of

_____ pecan pie. If you picked mostly *c*'s, you can't say no to
  ADJECTIVE

a heaping _____ of pumpkin or sweet potato pie!
              NOUN

From TURKEY TIME MAD LIBS® • Copyright © 2013, 2025 by Penguin Random House LLC

MAD LIBS® is fun to play with friends, but you can also play it by yourself! To begin with, DO NOT look at the story on the page below. Fill in the blanks on this page with the words called for. Then, using the words you have selected, fill in the blank spaces in the story.

Now you've created your own hilarious MAD LIBS® game!

EXCERPT FROM A THANKSGIVING PAGEANT

_____ ADJECTIVE

_____ NOUN

_____ ADJECTIVE

_____ PLURAL NOUN

_____ SOMETHING ALIVE (PLURAL)

_____ ADJECTIVE

_____ ANIMAL (PLURAL)

_____ TYPE OF EVENT

_____ PLURAL NOUN

_____ ADJECTIVE

_____ TYPE OF FOOD (PLURAL)

_____ ADJECTIVE

_____ EXCLAMATION

_____ TYPE OF FOOD

_____ ADJECTIVE

EXCERPT FROM A THANKSGIVING PAGEANT

This is a/an _____ scene from a children's Thanksgiving
                    ADJECTIVE
_____ pageant. This scene can be read aloud by two
      NOUN
_____ _____.
 ADJECTIVE   PLURAL NOUN

Pilgrim #1: Welcome to the first Thanksgiving, our dear friends and

_____!
SOMETHING ALIVE (PLURAL)

Pilgrim #2: We want to say a/an _____ thank-you to our fine
                                      ADJECTIVE
feathered _____, without whom this _____
           ANIMAL (PLURAL)   TYPE OF EVENT
would not be possible!

Pilgrim #1: And thank you to all the golden _____ we
                                                  PLURAL NOUN
grow in our fields! We appreciate having such a/an _____
                                                      ADJECTIVE
harvest.

Pilgrim #2: That's for sure. We can't wait to eat these tasty corn

_____! We are also thankful for all of our
 TYPE OF FOOD (PLURAL)

_____ friendships.
  ADJECTIVE

Pilgrim #1: _____! Let's eat this _____ before it
                EXCLAMATION   TYPE OF FOOD
gets _____!
      ADJECTIVE

From TURKEY TIME MAD LIBS® • Copyright © 2013, 2025 by Penguin Random House LLC

MAD LIBS® is fun to play with friends, but you can also play it by yourself! To begin with, DO NOT look at the story on the page below. Fill in the blanks on this page with the words called for. Then, using the words you have selected, fill in the blank spaces in the story.

Now you've created your own hilarious MAD LIBS® game!

WHAT IN THE GOURD?

PLURAL NOUN _____

PLURAL NOUN _____

ADJECTIVE _____

SOMETHING ALIVE (PLURAL) _____

TYPE OF FOOD (PLURAL) _____

ADJECTIVE _____

ADJECTIVE _____

ADJECTIVE _____

TYPE OF FOOD (PLURAL) _____

TYPE OF LIQUID _____

PLURAL NOUN _____

PLURAL NOUN _____

SOMETHING ALIVE (PLURAL) _____

VERB _____

NOUN _____

WHAT IN THE GOURD?

Gourds are funny little _____ often used to decorate
                         PLURAL NOUN

holiday _____ at Thanksgiving. But what *are* these
         PLURAL NOUN

_____ little _____? They may look like
 ADJECTIVE   SOMETHING ALIVE (PLURAL)

tiny pumpkins or miniature _____, but you don't
                            TYPE OF FOOD (PLURAL)

want to eat them. They smell _____ and they taste
                              ADJECTIVE

_____, too. Gourds are related to squash and pumpkins, and
 ADJECTIVE

they are considered a/an _____ fruit. But unlike those
                          ADJECTIVE

_____, they are used only for decoration or to store
 TYPE OF FOOD (PLURAL)

_____ or other _____. They are also often
 TYPE OF LIQUID   PLURAL NOUN

used as musical _____. Gourds sure are adorable
                 PLURAL NOUN

little _____, but look, don't _____,
        SOMETHING ALIVE (PLURAL)   VERB

when you see them on your Thanksgiving _____!
                                        NOUN

From TURKEY TIME MAD LIBS® • Copyright © 2013, 2025 by Penguin Random House LLC

TOM THE TURKEY

_____ SOMETHING ALIVE (PLURAL)

_____ TYPE OF CONTAINER

_____ PLURAL NOUN

_____ NOUN

_____ TYPE OF BUILDING

_____ PART OF THE BODY

_____ NOUN

_____ NOUN

_____ TYPE OF FOOD (PLURAL)

_____ NOUN

_____ PLURAL NOUN

_____ SOMETHING ALIVE

_____ PLURAL NOUN

_____ ADJECTIVE

_____ SAME SOMETHING ALIVE

_____ SAME TYPE OF BUILDING

MAD LIBS® is fun to play with friends, but you can also play it by yourself! To begin with, DO NOT look at the story on the page below. Fill in the blanks on this page with the words called for. Then, using the words you have selected, fill in the blank spaces in the story.

Now you've created your own hilarious MAD LIBS® game!

TOM THE TURKEY

On Christmas, _____ get visited by Santa Claus.
                SOMETHING ALIVE (PLURAL)

On Easter, the Easter Bunny hops into your _____.
                                           TYPE OF CONTAINER

But who comes to give you _____ on Thanksgiving?
                          PLURAL NOUN

Tom the Turkey, that's who! If you have been a thankful little girl or

_____, Tom the Turkey just might come visit your
      NOUN

_____ on Thanksgiving. While you rest your pretty
TYPE OF BUILDING

little _____ during your post-meal nap, this magical
       PART OF THE BODY

_____ flies through the _____ and leaves cornucopias
    NOUN   NOUN

filled with _____ at your front _____. Your
            TYPE OF FOOD (PLURAL)   NOUN

cornucopia might be filled with candy, presents, and _____,
                                                     PLURAL NOUN

if you're lucky. But if you've been an ungrateful little _____,
                                                         SOMETHING ALIVE

you'll get a cornucopia filled with _____! So be a/an
                                    PLURAL NOUN

_____ little _____, and maybe this year Tom
ADJECTIVE   SAME SOMETHING ALIVE

the Turkey will come to your _____!
                             SAME TYPE OF BUILDING

From TURKEY TIME MAD LIBS® • Copyright © 2013, 2025 by Penguin Random House LLC

MAD LIBS

World's Greatest Word Game

Want to keep laughing?
Check out these other Mad Libs books!

Download the awesome **FREE** Mad Libs app!

Available Now

A super silly way to fill in the _____!
PLURAL NOUN